Redouté

THE MAN WHO PAINTED FLOWERS

CAROLYN CROLL

G. P. PUTNAM'S SONS ✿ NEW YORK

In memory of my cousin
Kathi Rosen,
who loved painting flowers

With grateful thanks to:

Dr. William M. Klein, executive director of the National Tropical Botanical Garden, Lawai, Island of Kuai, Hawaii, for his letters of introduction to the botanical libraries of Paris and London.

Monsieur and Madame Laurent Delcourt and Abbé Prosper Chalon, Saint-Hubert, Belgium, for sharing their history and hospitality with me.

Sue Ann Houser, former co-director, W. Graham Arader III Gallery, Philadelphia, PA, for allowing me to surround myself with Redouté's watercolors and prints whenever I liked.

Madelaine, Joseph, and Michael Fox, Joseph Fox Books, Philadelphia, PA, for providing fertile ground where people and ideas come together and grow.

G. P. Putnam's Sons, Reg. U.S. Pat. & Tm. Off. Published simultaneously in Canada
Printed in Singapore. Book designed by Gunta Alexander. Text set in Bembo
Library of Congress Cataloging-in-Publication Data
Croll, Carolyn.   Redouté: the man who painted flowers / Carolyn Croll.   p.   cm.
1. Redouté, Pierre Joseph, 1759–1840—Juvenile literature. 2. Botanical artists—France—Biography—Juvenile literature. 3. Botanical illustration—France—History—Juvenile literature.
4. Flower painting and illustration—France—History—Juvenile literature.
[1. Redouté, Pierre Joseph, 1759–1840. 2. Artists.] I. Title. QK98. 183. R43C76   1995
582.13′04463′0222—dc20   [B]   93-42394   CIP   AC   ISBN 0-399-22606-0
1   3   5   7   9   10   8   6   4   2
First Impression

AUTHOR'S NOTE

I first glimpsed one of Pierre-Joseph Redouté's watercolors of roses at an exhibition of botanical art held at the Academy of Natural Sciences in Philadelphia some years ago. Its delicacy and freshness took my breath away, even though it had been painted more than 175 years before, and I was curious to know about the artist.

Reading about Redouté's life led me to travel to Saint-Hubert, Paris, Malmaison, and London to visit some of the places he knew. His single-minded determination to do something considered "small" in the art world but to do it perfectly touched my heart and stirred my imagination. I began to think about telling his story in words and pictures using the colors of his flowers and the design motifs of late-eighteenth- and early-nineteenth-century engravings.

I knew it wouldn't be possible to tell everything about his life in a picture book. Yet I hope what I've chosen will give you, the reader, a sense of Redouté's extraordinary times and his exquisite art.

Pronunciation Guide

Antoine-Ferdinand—an-TWAN fehr-di-NAHN
basilica—ba-SIL-i-ka
Benedictine abbey—ben-eh-DIK-teen AB-bee
botanist—BAH-ton-ist
Charles-Louis L'Héritier de Brutelle—sharl loo-EE lehr-ee-T'YAY de broo-TEL
Henri-Joseph—on-REE zho-ZEF
Jardin du Roi—zhar-DAN doo rwah
Malmaison—mahl-may-ZON
Marie Antoinette—ma-REE an-twa-NET
Pierre-Joseph Redouté—p'yair zho-ZEF ray-doo-TAY
portrait—POR-trit
Raphael—RAF-ah-el
Rembrandt—REM-brant
Saint-Hubert—san-too-BEAR
sou (old French coin)—soo
Versailles (French royal palace near Paris)—vair-SIGH

Bibliography

Anderson, Frank J. *The Complete Book of 169 Redouté Roses*. New York: Abbeville, 1979.

Diderot, Denis. *L'Encyclopédie* (Paris, 1752). New York: Dover, 1959.

Hobhouse, Penelope. *Gardening Through the Ages*. New York: Simon & Schuster, 1992.

Mallary, Peter and Frances. *A Redouté Treasury: 468 Watercolors from "Les Liliacées."* New York: Vendome, 1986.

Ridge, Antonia. *The Man Who Painted Roses*. London: Faber & Faber, 1974.

Rix, Martyn. *The Art of Botanical Illustration*. New York: Arch Cape, 1990.

———, and William T. Stearn. *Redouté's Fairest Flowers*. New York: Prentice-Hall, 1987.

———. *The Age of Napoleon: Costume from Revolution to Empire 1789–1815*. New York: The Metropolitan Museum of Art/Abrams, 1989.

No one in the Belgian village of Saint-Hubert was surprised that Pierre-Joseph Redouté wanted to be an artist when he grew up, because his father was a painter, just like *his* father and grandfather before him.

Papa Redouté painted decorations for the Benedictine abbey that stood next to the great basilica in the center of the village. And sometimes, to make ends meet, he painted portraits.

More than anything Papa Redouté wanted his sons to carry on the family tradition, so as soon as Antoine-Ferdinand and Pierre-Joseph and Henri-Joseph were old enough to hold a paintbrush, he began to teach them everything he knew.

"People pay well for pictures of themselves and things that happened long ago," Papa Redouté told his sons, and he sent them to school to learn reading, writing, and history.

But Pierre-Joseph wasn't interested in ancient battles and conquering heroes. He wanted to know all about the sweet-smelling herbs and flowers that grew in the abbey garden and in the woods surrounding Saint-Hubert.

Sick people came to the abbey from miles around to ask advice and get medicine that one of the monks made from the plants. The wise monk patiently taught Pierre-Joseph the names of all the plants, and told him which were poisonous and which could help cure sickness. He showed Pierre-Joseph the ancient books about plants kept in the abbey library. The pictures in the books were stiff and didn't look much like real flowers, but they gave Pierre-Joseph ideas.

When Pierre-Joseph made some flower pictures of his own, Papa Redouté saw them and shook his head. "No one will pay good money for flower paintings. Saints and heroes will make your fortune, my son."

As Pierre-Joseph reached his thirteenth birthday, there was nothing more that Papa Redouté could teach him. It was time for him to make his own way in the world, which was not unusual in those days. So Pierre-Joseph packed his paints and brushes and Papa Redouté gave him a letter of introduction to show to other painters he would meet along the way.

Pierre-Joseph walked from village to town to city. Often he was cold and hungry, but soon he began to find work. Sometimes he painted a picture just for supper and a place to sleep. If there was a master painter in the town, Pierre-Joseph showed him Papa's letter and the great man gave him lessons. Then Pierre-Joseph chopped wood or fetched water to repay his teacher.

Wherever he went, there was a lot to learn from the master-pieces in the churches and town halls. But the paintings that lifted his spirits and touched his heart were filled with flowers.

From then on, as he walked from place to place, Pierre-Joseph stopped to draw the wild flowers that grew in the meadows and along the country lanes. Soon these blossoms found their way into the portraits and Bible scenes he painted.

People liked young Redouté's pictures and his friendly country ways. He was busy all the time, painting portraits and whatever else they wanted him to paint, but he was not happy. I need to do what I love best, he thought sadly.

Then one day a letter came from his brother Antoine-Ferdinand. He wanted Pierre-Joseph to work with him in Paris painting scenery for the Italian opera.

Now there were lots of flowers for him to paint, though not exactly the sort Pierre-Joseph had in mind.

But he loved Paris, because there were many beautiful gardens there. When his work at the theater was finished for the day, Redouté went to the most beautiful garden of all, the Jardin du Roi, King Louis XVI's garden. Here, in the last few hours of daylight, he sat and drew *real* flowers.

It was not long before the king's gardeners became his friends. Just like the kind monk in Saint-Hubert, they answered his questions and were quick to show him any rare or especially lovely blossom.

One day a stranger watched the young man painting in the king's garden. He could tell from Redouté's pictures how much he loved flowers.

"How would you like to make the pictures for a book I am writing about some newly discovered plants?" the man asked. "You will work hard, but I will pay well."

This was a red-letter day for Redouté. The man was Charles-Louis L'Héritier de Brutelle, a first-class botanist who took the study of plants seriously. He taught Redouté to look closely at all the details, and the closer the young man looked at a flower the more he saw what a miracle it was.

Doing what he loved didn't seem at all like work to Redouté. And his new position meant he could now marry his dear Marie-Marthe. When their children were born, Redouté couldn't wait until they were old enough to hold a paintbrush so he could teach them everything he knew about painting flowers.

Monsieur L'Héritier took Redouté to London to meet famous scientists and artists of the day. Redouté learned a new way of printing copies of pictures, and he drew in the English king's garden at Kew.

When L'Héritier's book was published, many people bought it because they liked Redouté's beautiful drawings.

He was asked to paint flowers for the King's Vellums, the royal collection of paintings of French flowers and animals kept at Versailles. Then he was made flower painter to Her Majesty Queen Marie Antoinette. There wasn't any salary to go along with his new title, but Redouté was still proud.

But in 1789 prices and taxes were rising for everyone in France. Poor people were tired of starving while the king and queen lived in luxury. Many Frenchmen fought alongside the American colonists in their war for independence, and they thought France would also be better off without a king.

The angry mob took charge. The king and queen were arrested.

One night Redouté was ordered to bring his paints and brushes to the prison where the royal family was being held. He was frightened, thinking he too would be arrested.

Redouté was astonished when the queen asked him to paint a rare cactus that had bloomed just that night at midnight. This was the last time he saw Marie Antoinette; soon both she and the king were executed.

Ten years went by before the French people found a leader they could count on, General Napoleon Bonaparte.

Napoleon's wife, Josephine, loved beautiful things, especially flowers. While Napoleon brought law and order to France, she planted gardens at Malmaison, her country house. And when she asked her official botanist to write a book about her flowers, he sent for Redouté to make the pictures. Redouté had never been happier.

One day Napoleon came by and watched Redouté working. "With your talent, why waste your time painting pictures of flowers instead of great events in history?" the general asked.

"Painting flowers may be something small, but it is what I do best, because it is what I love most," Redouté answered politely.

By now, having drawn hundreds of pictures for other people's books, Redouté began work on one of his own. A book about lilies would be a big help to botanists, because the real flowers were hard to dry and keep for study. Redouté painted 486 lilies, each more beautiful than the last. All the work was done by hand, and the book took fourteen years to finish.

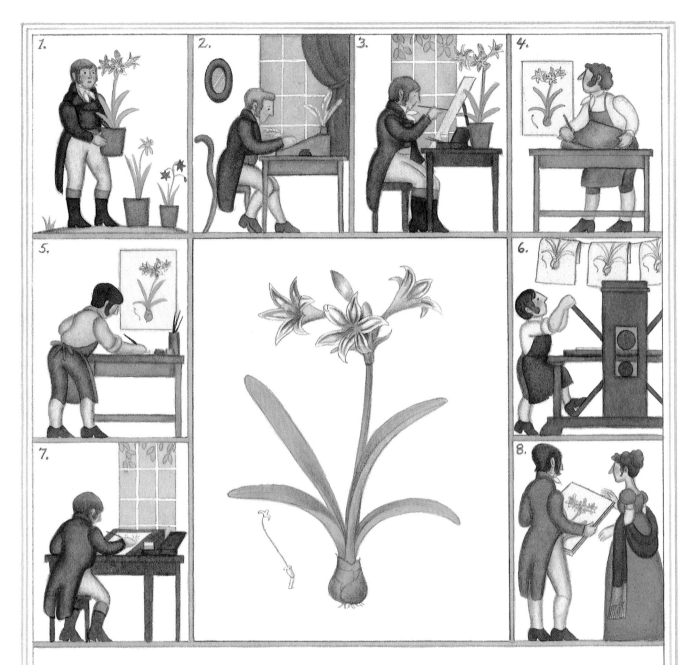

How Redouté Made His Book

1 · Redouté collected the flowers.
2 · Three botanists wrote the words.
3 · Redouté painted each lily, iris, and tulip with watercolors.
4 · An engraver copied each painting, scratching tiny dots onto a copper plate with a fine tool.
5 · The engraved plate was painted with colored inks.
6 · The printer put a sheet of paper on top and made a copy on his press.
7 · Some color was added to the prints by hand.
8 · People who bought the book received new pages every year for fourteen years.

Napoleon and Josephine gave copies of Redouté's book to kings and princes and libraries and museums all over Europe. They wanted people to see the glory of French art and science.

And when Napoleon and Josephine were crowned Emperor and Empress of France, Josephine made Redouté her official flower painter. This time the title came with a handsome salary and some trees for his garden. To Queen Marie Antoinette, Redouté was a servant; but to Empress Josephine, he was a friend.

Josephine and Napoleon had no children of their own, and the emperor, who wanted an heir, divorced her. In her sadness Josephine turned to her roses, which she had always loved. Seeing this, the faithful Redouté told her he was going to make a new book.

Redouté's family and friends helped him search for every kind of rose they could find. Some had never been named before, so they called them after good friends such as Monsieur L'Héritier and Empress Josephine. There was even one named after Redouté.

One day everyone at Malmaison became sad and worried. Empress Josephine was sick. She asked to see Redouté but told him not to come close for fear he might catch her sore throat. Two days later she died, and Redouté was beside himself with grief.

In his sorrow he kept on painting roses. He labored for seven years, and when he finished the book it was his masterpiece. People called Redouté the "Rembrandt of Roses" and the "Raphael of Flowers," after the renowned painters.

However, when Empress Josephine died, Redouté lost most of his income as well as his friend. With his head full of flowers, the generous Redouté had never given any more thought to money than he had to history. He had not saved a sou, and before long he was in debt.

To make matters worse, the new king of France did not care about art and science and did not want to impress anyone with expensive books about flowers. Marie-Marthe was worried.

But Redouté told her he was going to paint bouquets of the most beautiful flowers and fruits, not for botanists or the king this time, but for art lovers. And he taught the fashionable ladies of Paris to paint flowers. "Flowers are the stars of the earth and should be handled with tenderness and love," he told them.

One of his best students was Princess Marie-Louise, daughter of the duke of Orleans. Before the princess left to marry the king of Belgium, she painted a bouquet for her old teacher.

Redouté's fame spread far. The painter John James Audubon came to show Redouté his pictures of birds. Kind old Redouté introduced him to important friends who loved beautiful art and he gave Audubon some of his flowers to take back home to America.

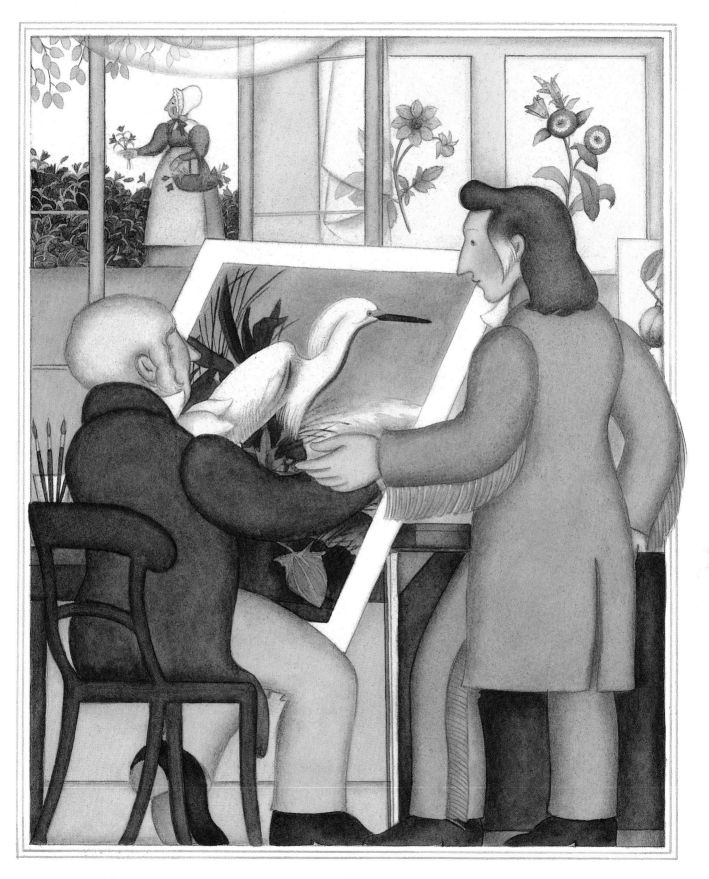

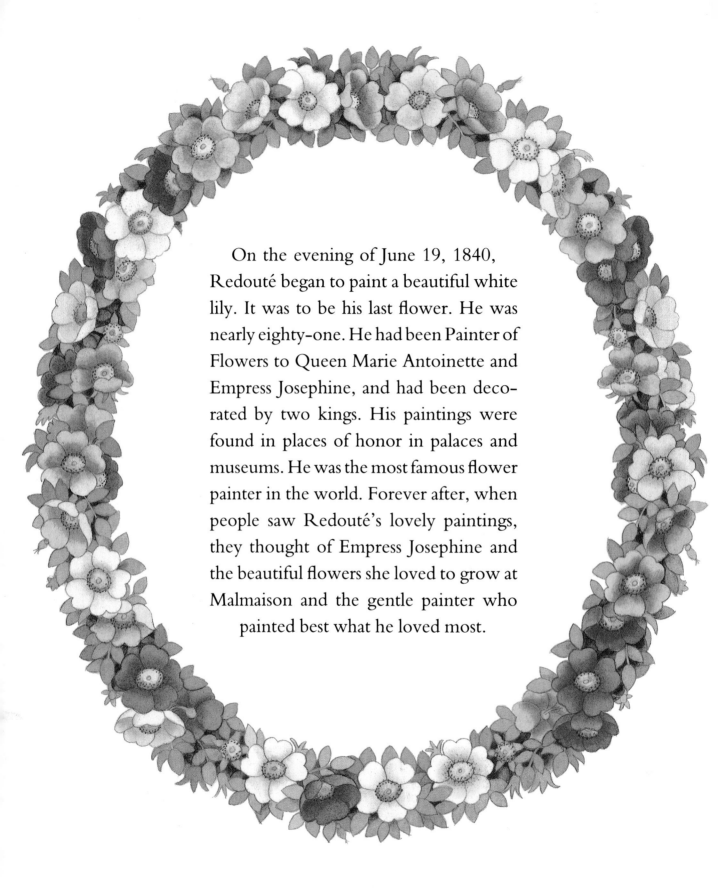

On the evening of June 19, 1840,
Redouté began to paint a beautiful white
lily. It was to be his last flower. He was
nearly eighty-one. He had been Painter of
Flowers to Queen Marie Antoinette and
Empress Josephine, and had been deco-
rated by two kings. His paintings were
found in places of honor in palaces and
museums. He was the most famous flower
painter in the world. Forever after, when
people saw Redouté's lovely paintings,
they thought of Empress Josephine and
the beautiful flowers she loved to grow at
Malmaison and the gentle painter who
painted best what he loved most.